Where's My Tail?

by Susan Schafer
Illustrated by Doug Cushman

Marshall Cavendish
New York • London • Singapore

Marshall Cavendish, 99 White Plains Road, Tarrytown, NY 10591
www.marshallcavendish.us
Library of Congress Cataloging-in-Publication Data

Schafer, Susan.
Where's my tail? / Susan Schafer ; illustrated by Doug Cushman.– 1st ed.
p. cm.
Summary: A small green lizard loses his tail while escaping a bobcat and,
unaware that it will grow back, asks a series of forest animals about
their tails and whether they will help find his.
ISBN 0-7614-5170-6
1. Lizards–Juvenile fiction. [1. Lizards–Fiction. 2. Tail–Fiction. 3. Forest animals–Fiction.]
I. Title: Where is my tail?. II. Cushman, Doug, ill. III. Title.

PZ10.3.S294Wh 2005
[E]–dc22
2004019317
The text of this book is set in Futura Book.
The illustrations are rendered in pen and ink, watercolors, and gouache.
Book design by Adam Mietlowski

Printed in China
First edition
1 2 4 6 5 3

To Paul, for laughing in the right places, and to
Cheyenne and Brooke Love, for being my best critics
—S.S.

To Turtle Bay in Redding, California
—D.C.

One day Little Lizard was sunbathing on his favorite rock. He had no idea that a bobcat was peering at him through the bushes.

Suddenly the bobcat spread her sharp claws and pounced. As Little Lizard dove into his hole, he felt a small tug from behind.

Little Lizard's heart, barely the size of an apple seed, thumped wildly. For the rest of the day and all through the night, he hid in his hole.

The next morning was sunny and bright. Little Lizard poked his nose into the air. There was no sign of the bobcat, so he climbed back onto his rock.

But when he turned around, he saw that his tail was gone!

"Where's my tail?" cried Little Lizard. He rushed back to his hole, but his tail wasn't there.

He searched around his rock, but all he found was a clump of moss and a snail shell.

"My tail must be somewhere! I'll have to keep looking for it," exclaimed Little Lizard. He skittered to the creek, where a chubby frog was squatting in the water. "Your tail is missing, too!" cried Little Lizard. "What happened to it?"

"Burrrrp, burrrp," said the frog. "I lost my tail a long time ago, when I changed from being a tadpole, and I don't want it back. It would weigh me down when I jump." And, with a big splash, the frog hopped away.

Little Lizard wandered farther along the creek.
He spotted a raccoon washing a fish for his lunch.
"What a bushy tail you have. Have you ever
lost it?" asked Little Lizard.

"Goodness, no," chattered the raccoon. "Without it, I'd be in big trouble. Its rings help me blend into shadows and hide from my enemies."

Since the raccoon wouldn't help him, Little Lizard scurried into the woods.

Soon he came upon a huge black bear taking a nap.
"Another animal without a tail!" he said. "Excuse me!"
he squeaked into the bear's ear.

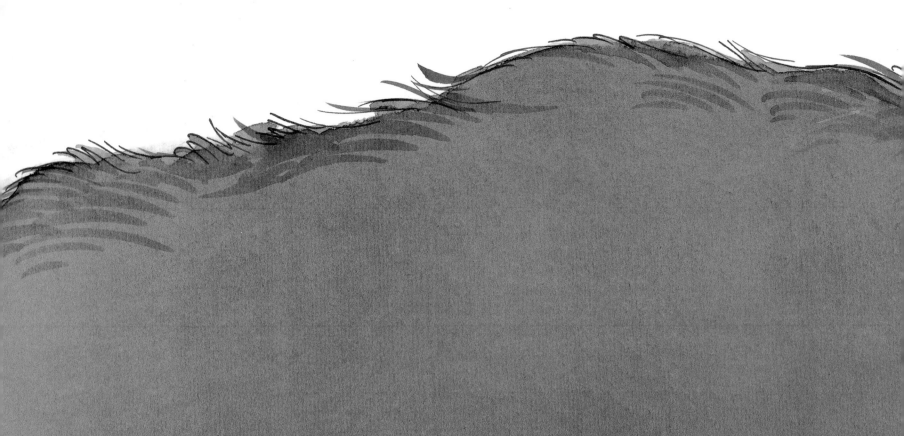

"**Rrrrrrrrrrrr,**" growled the bear. "You woke me up!"
"I'm sorry," said Little Lizard. "I'm looking for my tail.
Have you lost yours, too? I'll help you find it, if you help me
find mine."

"RRrrrrrRRRRR.

"My tail isn't missing. It's just stubby. Nobody insults me and gets away with it." The bear stomped toward Little Lizard.

But Little Lizard was quick. He dived under some leaves, and the bear lumbered off.

"I'll *never* find my tail!" moaned Little Lizard.

Just then a long, scaly tail dropped from a low branch.
"What a magnificent tail!" exclaimed Little Lizard.

An opossum, startled by the noise, fell from the tree
and crumpled into a heap.

"Yikes!" squeaked Little Lizard. "Are you all right?"

The opossum didn't move. Carefully, Little Lizard
poked him.

The opossum still didn't move.
Finally, he opened one beady eye.
"You're alive!" said Little Lizard, sighing with relief.
"Now, tell me, have you ever lost your tail?"

"I've had my tail since I left my mother's pouch," said the opossum. "I need it to grab on to branches when I'm climbing. Good day." With that, the opossum scrambled back up the tree.

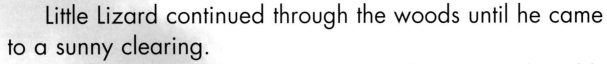

Little Lizard continued through the woods until he came to a sunny clearing.

"Pee-yew!" he cried. Something smelled oily and terrible.

A striped skunk with a twitchy black-and-white tail trotted toward him.

"Something stinks!" said Little Lizard.

"Humph," said the skunk. "That's no way to greet someone. I just sprayed a bear who was poking around my den. Look out! Here he comes!"

"Uh-oh," said Little Lizard, and he scampered away.
When he got back to the creek, he stopped to rest
on a fallen branch.
Suddenly the branch moved.

"**GET OFF!**" shouted the branch. Little Lizard jumped. He had been sitting on a gopher snake!

It was hard to tell where the snake's body ended and its tail began.

"You have enough tail for two animals!" cried Little Lizard. "Won't you share your tail with me?"

"Are you crazy?" said the snake. "I need all of my tail to climb and balance as I search for food. Sssssssay, I feel hungry right now."

Little Lizard didn't stick around to find out what the snake had in mind.

He ran all the way back to his favorite rock.

When he got there, he found a large green lizard sitting on top. "Oh no," said Little Lizard. "I've lost my tail and now my home."

"There's plenty of room for two," said the large lizard. "And don't worry about your tail. If it was grabbed by an enemy, it probably fell off."

Little Lizard remembered the bobcat.

"But most lizards grow new ones," continued the large lizard. "Turn around and look."

So that's exactly what Little Lizard did. And what do you think he saw?

A new tail!

The Tail End

Most lizards lose their tails when an enemy grabs them from behind. The tail breaks off and wiggles like a worm. The wiggling tail distracts the enemy while the lizard gets away. Like most lizards, Little Lizard grows a new tail. He is the only animal in the forest who can. But he meets other animals with tails that can do things that his tail can't. Here is some more information about those animals and their tails:

Adult **frogs** don't have tails, but tadpoles do. Tadpoles are newborn frogs. They live in the water and use their tails to swim, the way fish do. Their tails slowly shrink away as they change into adult frogs.

The mask on a **raccoon's** face and the rings on its tail blend into the shadows of the forest and make raccoons hard to spot. Raccoons use their tails for balance when climbing, for support when sitting up, and as warm wraps when sleeping. The tails also store fat, which raccoons need to stay alive in the cold winter months.

A **bear's** tail is a short, furry flap that covers and protects the bear's bottom. The tail acts like a small pillow so the bear can sit comfortably on the ground or on the rough branches of trees.

An **opossum's** tail is naked and scaly like a rat's. Opossums use their tails to hang on to branches as they climb. When threatened, an opossum bares its teeth and hisses. If it gets really frightened, it "plays dead."

When a **skunk** is disturbed, it stands on its front feet and lifts its tail high in the air. The tail is like a warning flag, telling an enemy to get away. If the enemy ignores the warning, the skunk sprays a stinky liquid from under its tail into the enemy's face.

It's hard to tell where a **snake's** body ends and its tail begins. That's because snakes don't have legs. A snake's tail starts behind its vent. The vent is the opening where wastes leave the body. It is located near the end of the snake, on its underside.